DON'T FORGET

Patricia Lakin

DON'T FORGET

PICTURES BY

Ted Rand

ALADDIN PAPERBACKS

New York   London   Toronto   Sydney   Singapore

First Aladdin Paperbacks edition March 2002
Text copyright © 1994 by Patricia Lakin Koenigsberg
Illustrations copyright © 1994 by Ted Rand

Aladdin Paperbacks
An imprint of Simon & Schuster
Children's Publishing Division
1230 Avenue of the Americas
New York, NY 10020

10 9 8 7 6 5 4 3 2 1

The Library of Congress has cataloged the hardcover edition as follows:
Lakin, Pat. Don't forget/by Patricia Lakin; pictures by Ted Rand.—1st ed. p. cm.
Summary: While buying the ingredients for her first cake—a surprise for her
mother's birthday—Sarah shares secrets with the friendly neighborhood
shopkeepers, especially with the Singers, who have blue numbers on their arms.
[1. Holocaust survivors—fiction. 2. Jews—United States—fiction.
3. Cake—Fiction.] I. Rand, Ted, ill. II. Title.
PZ7.L1586Dm 1994 [E]—dc20 93-20341 CIP AC
ISBN 0-688-12075-X.—ISBN 0-688-12076-8 (lib. bdg.)
ISBN 0-689-84809-9 (Aladdin pbk.)

Reprinted by arrangement with Aladdin Paperbacks, an imprint of
Simon & Schuster Children's Publishing Division.
Printed in the U.S.A.

*For my two sons, Aaron and Benjamin, with hopes that
their world will cease to condemn others based on religion,
sexual preference, nationality, or color of skin.
I would also like to thank Ruth Levine for sharing her
thoughts, and Amy Hest for sharing her talents.*
P. L.

Sarah pocketed her money and folded up her list. If only she could find a way not to shop at Singer's.

She ran down Sonoma Street and turned left at the bottom of the hill. Blue Hill Avenue was filled with shops and people and the languages of the street . . . Yiddish, English, and even Russian too.

"What's the hurry?" Lazar the greengrocer said as he tipped his cap.

"I've lots to buy," said Sarah. "I need an orange, please." She showed him her list and the recipe. "I have a secret. I'm making a cake for Mama."

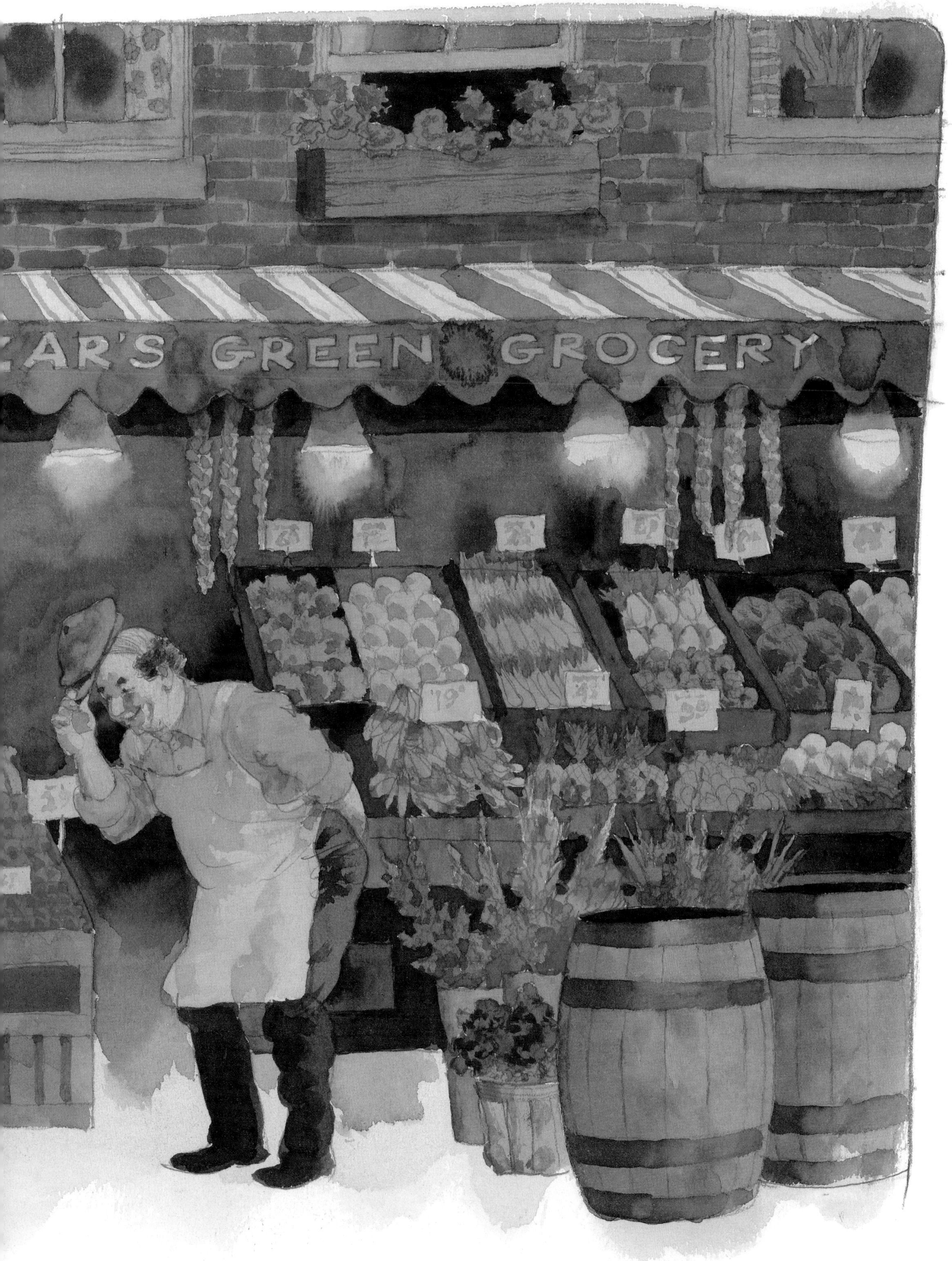
ZAR'S GREEN GROCERY
19¢

"Oy, so big," he sighed. "Too big for a nice half sour?"

"Never!" Sarah answered.

He pulled a pickle from a barrel and put an orange in a bag.

"Now I'll tell you *my* secret. For perfect sponge cake," he said, "never peek in the oven until it's done. My Mama taught me that."

"Never peek," said Sarah.

"Don't forget," said Lazar.

Sarah ate her pickle as she walked along the street. She stopped when she caught the smell of baking bread.

"How about some warm challah?" asked Mrs. Koretsky. "It goes good with pickle."

"Yes, please!" Sarah followed the baker inside.

"I need your best cake flour." Sarah checked her list. "Just two cups. And baking powder, two cups of sugar, and half a dozen eggs. That's everything I need!"

"Baking powder, sugar, and eggs? You'll have to go to Singer's for that."

The Singers were nice. But their secret was not.

"What's your Mama baking today?"

"Not Mama. Me," said Sarah. "I have a secret. I'm making my first cake—orange sponge."

"Then I'll tell you *my* secret, taught to me by my Papa, the best baker in all of Kiev! For perfect sponge cake," she whispered, "whip the egg yolks."

"Whip the yolks," repeated Sarah.

"Don't forget," said Mrs. Koretsky.

Singer's store was down the street. Sarah knew not to stare at the blue numbers tattooed on the Singers' left arms.

The brass bells jingled when she opened their door.

Mr. Singer put down his paper and leaned on the counter. "Why Sarahla. Getting prettier every day. And where's your lovely Mama?"

Sarah kept her eyes on his gold-rimmed glasses.

"Mama's home. Tomorrow's her birthday and I'm baking a cake. I need to buy some things."

Mrs. Singer used her apron to dry her hands. "Eight and already you bake?"

Sarah moved her eyes to the fan that hung from the tin ceiling.

"This is my first. But Mama doesn't know. It's her birthday surprise." She took out her money and stared at her list.

"Herschel, are you listening?" asked Mrs. Singer. "Does this remind you of a long time ago?"

"It certainly does." He sighed.

Sarah didn't think the Singers talked about long ago. That was when the Nazis gave them the blue numbers and put them in the concentration camp—just because they were Jews.

Mr. Singer held out his arm to reach for Sarah's list. His numbers were like magnets and drew her eyes right to that spot. 8 0 4 6 3.

When she looked up at the two of them, she knew they'd seen her stare.

"Come," Mrs. Singer took Sarah by the hand. She led her to the kitchen in the back.

"I'm sorry," said Sarah.

"Why? What have you done?"

"The numbers," said Sarah. "I tried not to stare."

"Ah, the numbers." Mrs. Singer held her arm out. "The numbers."

"I know how you got them. And that they are your secret."

"The numbers should *never* be a secret, my little Sarahla. If no one knows about bad things, they can happen all over again. Don't forget." She gave Sarah a hug. "But, you have a happy secret. You're making your Mama's birthday cake. And I have a present for you." She reached up into the cabinet and brought down an old cake pan.

"Thank you," said Sarah.

"I was older than you when I made *my* first cake in this pan—
and also without my Mama knowing," she told Sarah. "And if I
say so myself, it was good!"

"Was it for your Mama's birthday?"

"No, for a handsome young man from the next village. And, oh,
what a sweet tooth he had." She rubbed the rim of the pan. "You
see, making a cake in this very pan is how I caught Mr. Singer. So
for a perfect cake, kiss the pan before it goes in the oven."

"Kiss the pan," repeated Sarah.

"Don't forget," said Mrs. Singer.

Sarah took the pan and headed for the door.

"I forgot!" Sarah called.

"So soon?"

"The stove!" said Sarah. "I can't light it by myself. And if I ask Mama, she'll know the secret."

"Make your cake here, Sarahla. You have everything you need. But first, call your Mama. Tell her you're with us."

Mrs. Singer placed her mixer on the kitchen table.

"Did your Mama find out about your first cake?"

"I never had the chance to tell her," Mrs. Singer said softly.

Sarah whipped the egg yolks, added the sugar, orange juice, water, and flour. She beat the egg whites and folded them into the batter. Then she kissed the pan before it went into the oven. And she didn't peek, not even once.

Sarah shared her challah and they talked till the timer rang.
"Perfect," said Mrs. Singer after she tested the cake.
She packed it in a box and walked Sarah to the door.
The brass bells jingled as Mrs. Singer said, "Be sure to tell your Mama you made this cake by yourself."
"By myself," smiled Sarah.
"Don't forget," said Mrs. Singer.
"I won't," said Sarah. "I know I won't forget."

FRESH
EGGS
35¢ doz

SARAH'S FIRST CAKE
Orange Sponge Cake

6 eggs, separated and at
   room temperature
2 cups sugar
1/2 cup orange juice
rind of one orange, grated
1/2 cup of boiling water
2 cups cake flour, sifted
2 tsp. baking powder

Preheat oven to 325°.

Whip the egg yolks well while gradually adding 1 cup of sugar. Add the orange juice, orange rind, and water to the mixture. Sift the flour and baking powder together, adding it to the egg mixture by hand.

In a separate bowl beat the egg whites while gradually adding the remaining sugar. When stiff peaks form, gently fold the egg whites into the batter a little at a time. Pour into a 10″ *ungreased* angel-food pan. Bake for 20 minutes at 325°. Then increase to 350° for 35 minutes or until a toothpick inserted into the center comes out clean. Do not open the oven and peek before it's time.

Invert the pan on a rack for one hour and let it cool. Then loosen the sides with a cake spatula, remove, and put it on a cake plate. It's now ready to decorate.

For an extra special cake, kiss the pan before putting it in the oven.